MW00768951

I Mother
Is Another Word For
Love

_____

GIVEN TO

_____

OCCASION

_____

DATE

She speaks wise words.
And she teaches others to be kind.
She watches over her family.
And she is always busy.

Proverbs 31:26–27

It's 3 a.m. and your child is crying in the night. Without a second thought, you are by his side, giving him sips of soda and a few saltines to soothe the aches and pains of his sickness. Or you are in the kitchen cooking dinner for what seems to be the millionth time, when in she walks, tears streaming down her face. Everything stops as you, Mom, listen to her hurting heart and help her with your words of wisdom. These and countless others are the acts of love you have demonstrated throughout our lives, and now it's time you knew how much we, your children, appreciate you.

For all mothers who ever were or will be, *Mother Is Another Word For Love* is for you. It is to celebrate you. To champion your cause—your day-in, day-out devotion to your family and the community around you. Charming characters from Sam Butcher's collection capture the beautiful portrait you have spent so many years painting for us—the picture of Christ's undying, unwavering love for His family. May this book warm your heart as you do ours.

A Mother Is...

Loving

Love...patiently
accepts all things.
It always trusts,
always hopes, and
always continues
strong.

1 Corinthians 13:7

A Mother Is...

Nurturing

But we were very
gentle with you.
We were like a mother
caring for her little
children.

1 Thessalonians 2:7

A Mother Is...

Gentle

Let all men see that you are gentle and kind.

Philippians 4:5

A Mother Is...

Faithful

Love the Lord,
all you who belong
to him. The Lord
protects those who
truly believe.

Psalm 31:23

A Mother Is...

Resourceful

My God will use
his wonderful riches
in Christ Jesus to
give you everything
you need.

Philippians 4:19

A Mother Is...

Kind

Love each other like

brothers and sisters.

Give your brothers and

sisters more honor

than you want

for yourselves.

Romans 12:10

A Mother Is...

Godly

Raise them with
the training and
teaching of
the Lord.

Ephesians 6:4

A Mother Is...

Forgiving

Be kind and loving to each other. Forgive each other just as God forgave you in Christ.

Ephesians 4:32

A Mother Is...

Caring

But the wisdom that comes from God is like this: First, it is pure. Then it is also peaceful, gentle, and easy to please.

James 3:17

A Mother Is...

Patient

We must not become
tired of doing good.
We will receive our
harvest of eternal life
at the right time.
We must not give up!

Galatians 6:9

A Mother Is...

Persevering

Because you have
these blessings, you should ...
add these things to your lives:
to your faith, add goodness;
and to your goodness,
add knowledge; and to your
knowledge, add self-control;
and to your self-control,
add the ability to hold on.

2 Peter 1:5-6

A Mother Is...

Beautiful

Your beauty
should come from
within you—the beauty
of a gentle and quiet
spirit...is worth
very much
to God.

1 Peter 3:4

A Mother Is...

Diligent

She watches

over her family.

And she is

always busy.

Proverbs 31:27

A Mother Is...

Praiseworthy
Her children
bless her.
Her husband also
praises her.

Proverbs 31:28

A Mother Is...

Strong

I love you, Lord.

You are my

strength.

Psalm 18:1

A Mother Is...

Sharing

Share with

God's people who

need help.

Romans 12:13

A Mother Is...

A Healer

And the prayer
that is said with faith
will make the sick
person well.
The Lord will
heal him.

James 5:15

A Mother Is...

Thankful

Thank the Lord

because he

is good.

Psalm 107:1

A Mother Is...

Wise

Happy is
the person who
finds wisdom.

Proverbs 3:13

A Mother Is...

Prayerful
Be joyful because
you have hope.
Be patient when
trouble comes.
Pray at all times.

Romans 12:12

A Mother Is...

Serving

Each of you received

a spiritual gift....

So be good servants

and use your

gifts to serve

each other.

1 Peter 4:10

A Mother Is...

Blessed

"From now on,
all people will say
that I am blessed,
because the Powerful
One has done great
things for me."

Luke 1:48–49

I thank God every time I remember you.

Philippians 1:3

As a child, it just seemed automatic. Got a problem? Go tell Mom. Feeling sick? She'll help you feel better. Need some TLC? She's the one. No matter where we went or what we did, we always knew your love would follow. But as the years went by, a new realization dawned. Unbridled devotion is difficult to find. Other versions of love are often entangled in strings of expectation.

It is then we remember. Then we appreciate all the long hours, the sacrifices, the simple ways and big ways that Mom always said, "I love you...no strings attached." And we turn to God who gave us our mothers and marvel at His grace in giving us such precious—and yet so often unrecognized—treasures. Thank you, Mom, for living out the tender mercies of God before our very eyes. You have changed our lives forever, and we will always love you for the wonderful gift you've given us over and over again—you.